Alyssa's Lost Beauty

Written by: Christopher C. Smith

2

Christopher C. Smith

Father, Author, Actor, Independent Publisher & Song Writer

Special Thanks to

Emerald & The Eric Garner Foundation

Thank you's & Dedications

First I would like to give thanks to god

My Beautiful Mother
Ora Henderson

My Beautiful Daughter
Lauren Madison Smith

My Supportive Family

My Beautiful sister Valerie Hayes,
My niece Valyn
My nephews Vashon and D.J.
Cash Blocka & the B.G.G
Thanatos & my Canada family
Manny and the libraries
Damarkus Christmas & Darrell Washington
Ryan Levin & 4sure ent.
Shacora Johnson
Reyes Young
Christopher Bullock
D.J. Speak Eazy & G-Five
Hell Rell & The Whole Top Gunnas Family
The whole Yonkers & Bronx Family
Moe Dirdee,
Nikki & Amy, My whole Detroit Family
Every Body at the Wal-Mart #5404 Store

Areal BIG thanks to Cindy and the entire

"Little Company of Mary" hospital

for allowing me to do my first

"Achieving Our Dreams" Toy Drive
And thanks to Wal-Mart for the Sponsor!

Chapter 1

RING RING!!!!

I yawned loudly and stretched as I sat up in the bed to turn off my alarm clock. I couldn't help but hold the bandage that covered my scar on my lower stomach from the surgery as well as notice a nauseous feeling.

"Wow," I think to myself, "it really feels good to be home knowing I been in the hospital for quite some time now."

While placing my feet down on my cold bedroom floor, I looked back and began to smile. The same guy I had a huge crush on for all this time was now laying in my bed sleep.

"Charles! Charles, wake up! It's time for school and we're going to miss the bus," I said in a soft tone. But that was not working so I raised my voice and spoke more forcefully.

"Wake up boy!" Charles opened one eye and wiped the drool from his mouth.

"What time is it babe?" Charles asked with a slight smile, "Is it time to go already?"

"Yes, it is," I replied, "Now please get up before we end up having to walk to school. My parents left for work about an hour ago."

"Ok babe, here I come!" Charles said as he began to get ready for school.

We barely made it to the bus stop before the bus pulled up. While slowly walking on the bus with his head held low, Charles started to read a text message out loud to himself. It was from a baseball recruiter regarding his future. He had been working so hard throughout his high school years which made receiving this message extra exciting. In actuality, Charles was so thrilled he did not realize he was stopping the other teens from boarding the bus.

"Come on, now! What's the holdup?" One kid said with an angry voice. "Let's go, we don't have all day!"

Charles sat beside me and I could tell something was up. When we arrived at school I finally decided to ask.

"Hey, Charles, what's all the excitement about?"

We had walked all the way to our lockers before he completely answered my question. He told me that the greatest moment of his life is coming sooner than expected and that there will be a recruiter from one of his favorite teams, the Smithville Cougars, at his next game which was a couple days away. It was obvious that a congratulations was in order but suddenly, the nauseous feeling from when I woke up had returned.

"Umm, Charles? I will be right back," I said nervously as I then ran straight into the women's restroom.

I dashed into the first stall I saw open. Then I held my stomach as I started to throw up.

"This has to be a side effect from one of the medicines or something I ate last night for dinner." I thought to myself.

"Are you okay in there?" Charles screamed to me from outside the doors.

"Yeah, I'm fine! And *must* you be so loud?" I replied jokingly as I hurried out of the stall. I washed my hands and face then fixed my clothes and hair as if nothing happened before exiting the restroom.

"Oh, ol' okay! Just making sure, my *Sweet Sugar Plumps*."

"Umm, stop! Who is that I may ask?" I questioned while raising an eyebrow and screwing up my face.

Charles chuckled, "That's my new nickname for you!"

"Whatever," I replied as we made our way down the hall.

I was double checking my blouse to make sure I did not vomit on it anywhere when I felt a subtle tap on my shoulder. It was my best friend Ashley who I had known since the 7th grade. I had not seen her since the year before so it caught me by surprise.

"What are you two love birds talking about now?" she teased while giving me a hug.

"Well, Charles has a pretty big game coming up this weekend. A couple of recruiters will be there to check him out. You should come!" I invited.

"Oh wow! That's pretty awesome," Ashley commended with a shocked look on her face. "I never knew you were that good. I'm proud of you and of course, I'll be there!"

"Thanks" Charles replied.

Turning her attention back to me, Ashley stated, "Well! Y'all know this is my first day, right? Can you help me find my first class?"

"No doubt! Let me see your schedule," I answered. She handed over her roster and my eyes lit up. Ashley, Charles and I would all share the same schedule for the semester. This was dope.

"Wow! Looks like you can follow us because we all have the same classes! Yay!" We both cheered a little until our moment was interrupted by Charles.

"Cool. Well let's hurry up and get there. I would not want to be late," he suggested. Then he talked us through a stupor as he went on and on about his big game and how he wanted to make sure he was at his best throughout all of our periods. Before I knew it, I looked down at my watch and there were only 15 minutes before the final bell to go home.

By the time we loaded the bus, all of Charles' excitement and anticipation was running through me. Just hearing him rant about what he has to do to get prepared and how important his next game was showed how dedicated he is and how much he deserved everything that was happening for him.

"So, Babe, what are you doing once you get home?" I questioned seductively in a slight attempt to finally change the subject.

He gave me a strange look and then looked me up and down, licking his lips before he smiled. Then he replied, "Hmm. I don't know. But I do have to do more exercise and make sure that I'm fit and in shape because I can't hit home runs and not be able to run around the bases at top speed," and other randomness surrounding baseball.

As he chatted, I sat and listened with more amazement. I could not help but giggle a little at his thoroughness and realize I was falling more in love with him than I already had before.

"Can you come by my house today?" Charles suggested suddenly.

I was caught off guard in my own thoughts, "Hmmm, I got to ask--" I started but the bus driver yelled for the next person to get off at the top of his lungs interrupting me.

"Well, I guess not then," I said, giggling and before we knew it, it was time for Charles to get off the bus. The bus creeped in front of his house slowly before it came to a silent halt.

"Okay, I will see you later, Sugar Plumps," Charles said with a wink as he reached over to kiss me on my lips while rushing to get off the bus. I really did not want him to go without me so I quickly reached for his face and kissed him once more before he left. I started to blush as my cheeks turned rosy red, I couldn't help but notice how my heart then skipped a beat.

As Charles made it off the bus and headed toward his house he glanced back at me and blew a kiss. I giggled and pretended to catch it and placed it in my shirt pocket. I watched Charles chuckle and stumble his way into the house before the bus creeped away. It had not made it to the next stop sign before I text him "I love you" and within seconds he replied, "I love you too".

As I entered the front door of my home I could not help but notice the delicious smell that filled the air. It stopped me from heading straight to my room and to visiting the kitchen just to see what exactly the aroma was. To my surprise it was my favorite, meatloaf and cabbage.

"Hi dear," my mom said with an enthusiastic quirk about her, "How was your day?"

"Hey Mom," I replied. "It was cool. Where is Dad?" I said while looking around nervously.

"Oh, he will be right back! He went outside to take out the trash and run to the store down the street."

"Oh ok, cool!"

I sat my books down, washed my hands at the sink and started to make a plate. I heard my dad entering the back door with my dog shortly after. It seemed as though they both tried to race to enter the house at the same time forcing my dad to misstep and luckily catch himself on the refrigerator door. Needless to say I laughed but mainly due to the frustration and ill expression that now plagued my father's face, knowing he was upset because he almost fell.

When he finally noticed me I laughed even louder.

"Hi Dad!" I blurted out before he could say anything.

"Hi Alyssa, how was your day?" he questioned while limping his way over to my mom. He grabbed her hands from the stove, turned her around and gave her a kiss which was may too much affection for my eyes. The disturbing sight forced me to interrupt them.

"Um…. Excuse me? Please! Your child is here trying to enjoy a nice meal" I stated with little humor. They stopped tonguing each other down abruptly as if momentarily they both actually forgot where they were.

"Oh Lord, sorry about that," my mom uttered as she sat down at the table and crossed her legs. "Here is your plate Mr. Smith, now come on sit down and eat."

"Why, thanks Patricia," my dad said with a sarcastic tone. He wobbled to the table, sat down and proceeded to continue our conversation.

"So, Alyssa how is Charles? What did you guys do in school?"

"He is fine," I said. Then I stopped eating to fill my parents in about the exciting news he received earlier today. I also told them about the strange nausea I was feeling when I woke up and how I barely made it to the restroom to throw up.

"I have no idea what's wrong," I confessed.

"Could be the medicine you're taking? Or maybe the food you're eating?" My mom swiftly suggested.

"Yeah, I really have no clue, Mom," I said with a worried look on my face.

"Well, look at it this way, I'm pretty sure you're not pregnant," my dad said with a grunt and stuffing his face.

"Why would you even say something like that" my mom asked angrily. An awkward silence overcame the room as we just stared at each other.

"Well, are you?" My dad questioned.

"Well, if anything pops," I said jokingly. "We would have to engage in sexual encounters in order for that to happen. You know, me and Charles are taking things one step at a time." Although I knew we messed around the night before. But never the less, I thought to myself that pregnancy could not be an option because we used protection.

I spent more time talking about Charles and his big game all while trying to change the subject from me possibly being pregnant.

My dad then interrupted me, "So how is the recovery from the surgery you had. Were there any complications?"

Relieved that there were no more questions about pregnancy, I answered him and finished up my plate.

"Is there any more food left?" I asked.

"Wow Alyssa!" My mom said shocked. "I never seen you eat that much, and so fast, a day of my life. You must have skipped lunch today." She then pointed towards the stove and counter where she had placed the extra food she had cooked.

"What did you do all day?" My dad then asked my mom.

"Well for starters, when you came home from work the house was completely clean and there were groceries in the fridge. The bills had also gotten paid I might add," my mom said with a sarcastic tone. She then rolled her eyes jokingly while then looking at me. "So dear, Alyssa, please go on about your day."

I shook my head in amusement, my mom was always being fly. Then I invited them both to Charles' big game this weekend.

"It would be an honor if you guys could both come and support him as well. You know, so it looks like he has a lot of supporters and seeing that his family will be there as well... You guys could meet his parents! And also, most important, please dress appropriate and do not embarrass me," I said jokingly. They laughed and agreed to come. I finished eating, cleaned my plate then headed upstairs to get ready for bed.

"Good night, Alyssa!" My mom yelled from down stairs as she began to clean up the rest of the kitchen with my dad.

CHAPTER 2

I was changing into my pajamas when I realized I did not have my cellphone. I quickly started to panic and ended up destroying my room while looking for it.

"Hey Alyssa! Your phone is down here going off," my dad hollered up the steps. I took a deep breath, then hurried down the stairs to retrieve my phone. I forgot that as soon as I came in the house I had let my phone charged down stairs next to the sofa.

"Thanks, Dad," I said with the stupidest smile on my face. I hastily took the phone from him and headed back upstairs and into bed to see what I had missed.

There were quite a few missed calls and texts, mainly from Charles and Ashley. I pressed the button to return Charles' call but to my surprise, at the very same moment, he was trying to call me as well. So his call was automatically answered instead.

"Hey Charles, what's up?" My voice lit up and the biggest smile was on my face even though I was trying to not seem as excited. Honestly, if he was to see how I looked at that moment, he would probably laugh and I would totally be embarrassed.

"What you up to?" He asked in a soothing voice. "I had called to let you know that I was thinking about you. This Beyoncé song called "Halo" came on the radio not too long ago. I was listening to the lyrics and it reminded me so much of you."

"Aww," I blushed, "Thanks!" I said as I continued to smile even harder.

"So whenever you hear that song, please only think about me, okay?" Charles suggested.

"I will," I replied with a more serious tone in my voice, "are you ready for your big day in a couple of days?"

"No lie, I'm kind of scared, confident and nervous at the same time," Charles said with a laugh. I was not sure how that was possible, however I kept that thought to myself. We talked for what seemed like a couple minutes more until I looked over at my clock on the wall and realized I have been on the phone with Charles for more than 3 ½ hours.

Bleep, bleep. "What's that noise?" Charles asked.

"Oh wow", I replied, "it's my phone and it's about to die so if anything I will talk to you in the morning at school. I love you!"

"Okay, I love you too." Charles quickly replied.

"Okay, bye! Good night! I will be listening to that song until I fall asleep."

"Okay," Charles said.

"Talk to you later, okay, good night!"

We both sat on the phone another five minutes being stubborn as neither one of us wanted to let the other go. So we stayed on the our ends, going back and forth saying good bye to each other until finally I said, "Okay! On the count of *three*, we both hang up. Okay?

"That's fine", Charles said while laughing. But this time we both began to count down and then we finally hung up. I grinned with love as I pulled the covers over my head. Then I quickly fell asleep to face sweet dreams.

As my day then started I could not help but think to myself how much my life had changed since I met Charles and the wonderful times we shared. Even though we had the same roster we did not spend every moment the day together. Still, he always managed to pop up with cute text messages and or sneak kisses whenever he could. Needless to say, any moment we were not together was accounted for once we were reunited.

I was walking down the hall toward our 5th period class with Ashley when I felt a slight tap on left my shoulder. I glanced to the left just to hear Charles laughing to my right. I shook my head and rolled eyes as I reached up for a hug. Charles then leaned in extra to kiss my lips, just a quick peck, then spun around abruptly running into the classroom as if we both were in a race to see who would get to their seat first.

While standing there stunned and confused I looked at Ashley and she started shaking her head as well. I giggled as I walked into the classroom after him.

"You are such a goofball!"

Of course Charles was already slouching down at his assigned desk with his hands behind his head.

"So what took *you* so long, Alyssa?" He smirked.

"Umm, okay! First of all, class didn't start and you cheated!" I said smiling but rolling my eyes defensively. I noticed Charles staring at me why sat next to him and attempted to get myself situated. But his eyes glaring at my every movement was making my heart quickly melt.

I smiled while blushing, "Babe! You mind?" He frowned his face a bit, squinting his eyes, then turned around to the front and pulled out his phone. The class bell rang and the teacher began her lesson. I acted like I was paying attention until I felt my pocket vibrate. Sneaking my phone out my jeans I saw a new message from Charles.

"No, I love every inch of you." It read, with a ton of heart-faced emoji.

I looked over at him as he looked back at me grinning. Which made me grin in return as I whispered, "I love you too."

Class was almost over when I could tell Charles' mind must have switched back into game mode. He seemed uneasy again, after all, he was still in preparation for his big day tomorrow.

"Are you okay," I asked quietly, "it looks like you really have a lot on your mind?"

24

Noticing I was obviously concerned he started to respond, "Well to be honest..."

Ring! Ring! Ring!

The bell to go home sounded stopping Charles midsentence. As we headed to our lockers to get ready to go home Charles began to explain the pressure on him as this might be his only big shot to make his childhood dreams come true.

"Alyssa, you have no idea. I can actually feel it in my veins. This is my calling from God and I really want to be successful not only for me but for my parents as well," he explained. "I want to be able to spoil them as they have tried to give me the world thus far, and they deserve to be spoiled now."

Charles went on about how serious it is that he shows up and show out tomorrow. He went more into the story of his family struggles and he was real. I could tell these were the memories that overshadowed the depth of his motivation. And the idea of possibly overcoming previous misfortunes was something he held dear to his heart.

His eyes were filled with tears that would not fall by the time we sat down on the school bus. I took a deep breath and reached over to hug him as a tear gently rolled down his cheek and on to my shirt.

"I'm so sorry Alyssa," Charles apologized, "it's just that I really want this. I also want to be able to give you the life you never had as well."

"Charles, I will always be here and so will your family. More than that, you are amazing so don't worry about anything else," I replied while looking him in the face and squeezing his hands with confidence. "Hey, matter of fact, let's get off at another stop and get some ice cream or pizza." I suggested. I did not want my man sad or in his feelings before the biggest day of his baseball career.

After taking a couple deep breaths Charles finally agreed and suggested a spot right up the street from his house that served really good food.

"Great. I will just text my mom now and let her know I will be coming ho me a little late."

Shortly after texting my mom the bus came to our stop. We quickly got off and started walking down the street to the pizza place Charles had recommended. As we got closer, it looked like the block was under construction, we had to take a detour, and go around back.

We proceeded to follow the sidewalk signs re-routing our initial path but once we reached the restaurant, I noticed the police officers that where standing near the entrance door.

"Hey! Where are you guys headed?" An officer said with a serious look on his face. "This place is closed."

I thought to myself he must be joking. I looked over in to the restaurant, the lights were still on and the sign in the front window brightly read, "Open".

"What do you mean, Sir?" Charles said with a concerned look on his face. "The sign says, 'Open' and there are people sitting down inside, eating."

I could sense a terrible tension growing between Charles and the officer as they made eye contact. I quickly proposed that we went somewhere else to eat.

"No!" Charles said. "This place said it's open and there are people here, so *we* are going to eat here, no matter what anybody says!"

"Excuse me, Boy?" The officer said, now walking towards Charles. This made me more uncomfortable than I was before.

"Look Charles, let's just go!" I said with a scary tone as my voice began to shake.

"No!" Charles refused.

"What did you say?" The officer said getting into Charles' face. They were so close they bumped chests. "I will have you arrested for trespassing," he shouted.

Putting aside his pride and backing down Charles then looked at the officer's badge. "Hmmm. No, that's cool, Officer Norman", Charles said with a smirk on his face as they both walked away, staring at each other.

"You're crazy," I said, "you could've gotten arrested and put in jail back there!" I spoke with a serious and aggressive tone. Charles was looking down with his fist balled tight as if he was ready to swing on someone. By the looks of it, this was not the first time he encountered this same officer.

"I hate that guy! I swear, oh! I hate that guy" Charles repeatedly stated.

"Babe, let's just head home and you can tell me all about it."

"Okay, that's fine", Charles agreed, "but, do you think you could spend the night? My people just left for out of town earlier today."

"I will ask my mom after I get to your place." We continued to the three minute walk in silence.

After arriving at Charles' place I sat down on the couch looking up at him and asked if how he was feeling.

"Are you okay?" I questioned.

"Yes, I'm fine," Charles responded angrily. "I just can't believe that officer just tried to assault me like that."

"I know, babe," I agreed as I tried to comfort him, "he was a jerk! Did you get a chance to take down his name and badge number?" I held his hand to sit him down then helped him take off his jacket while caressing his shoulders.

"Well I did get his name but I couldn't really see his badge number," he answered in a less irritated tone.

"That's fine. As long as you remember the name we have a start. If anything, let's just cool down for a moment," I insisted. So we sat in silence a few minutes.

"Umm, Charles, where are your parents again?" I asked.

"Oh, them? Who needs them?" Charles replied jokingly then took his statement back. "Nah, they will be home in a couple days. They both are out of town. Left me the car to get to the game and everything."

"They won't be there?" I cut him off. Charles shook his head no and looked down at his hands. I felt sad, "Well, my parents said they will come if it means anything. Speaking of which, let me text my mom that I'm here."

I stood up to reach in my pocket and grab my phone. As I sent my mom the message, Charles raised from the couch. I could tell we had struck another nerve as he then began to walk back and forth across his living room.

"Hmm, so what did you want to do? Do you have any movies that we can watch?"

"Yeah, just look in the case by the television", Charles said with a calmer tone. "Were you able to get a hold of your parents to see if they will allow you to spend the night?" He asked.

"I did but now I'm waiting on my mom's response," I answered while glancing over the family's DVD collection.

Within instants, I felt a warm sensation come over my neck. Charles wrapped his arms around me and continued to kiss the back of my neck. I turned around to face him as I kissed him in return, passionately on his lips. He pulled me closer and we stumbled slowly onto the couch.

My hands caressed his back while he hovered over top of me kissing me everywhere. As the situation became more intimate Charles grabbed my hand and whispered, "Come on," in my ear.

I followed him without hesitation, stripping off his shirt as we stumbled up the stairs. Charles opened his room door directing me to walk in first with one hand while the other reached for my pants zipper. He closed the door with his foot as he proceeded to remove my clothes.

And then his phone rang.

And we stopped.

CHAPTER 3

"Hello, who am I speaking with?"
Charles answered nervously.

"Hi, this is Edward, recruiter on behalf of
the Smithville Cougars. We are looking
forward to meeting you at the game
tomorrow. We hope to see you at your
best."

"No problem, Sir! I will definitely bring my
'A' game plus more", Charles said as he
glanced at me. His face shown the
biggest smile I witnessed all night.

"Ok, well that's good to hear. Rest up, and
I will see you tomorrow," Edward said before
he hung up.

"Who was that?" I asked sarcastically.

"That was the recruiter from the
Smithville Cougars letting me know he'll
be at the game tomorrow."

"I am so proud of you," I said happily as I
leaned toward Charles and we started
kissing again. Finishing where we left off.

We laid next to each other under the
covers—naked and breathless—for a

while before a feeling, similar to butterflies throwing a rave in my stomach surfaced. Charles was so comfortable with his arms wrapped around me but I needed an excuse to get up.

"Babe, have you seen my phone?" I asked as I slowly raised his arm over my head and crept out the bed. I tiptoed around the room looking under random objects as if I was trying to retrace my steps. After a moment of admiring my now awkward walk and secretly giggling, Charles finally directed me downstairs.

"Look by the DVDs or couch, Alyssa."

"Oh, that's right!"

I threw on one of his T-shirts and shorts to go get my phone from off the charger. As expected, there were missed calls and several texts messages from my parents, just seeing if I was okay and letting me know it was fine that I stayed.

I began to reply to a text when my dad called.

"Hey Dad," I said calmly. He wasted no time as he immediately bombarded me with questions regarding Charles' big game. Most importantly, he wanted to know whether he needed to pick me up or should he and mom just meet us there to show their support.

"Thanks Dad," I finally responded, "I have a ride but I'm sure he would really enjoy you all coming."

I continued to give him the other information he requested until my mom snatched the phone to talk to me.

"Hi Mom," I giggled. "How was your day?"

She rushed through a laundry list of tasks she completed throughout the day then asked about my day as well. She exaggerated her concern for my being sick and vomiting and if I needed to come home, they would come and get me.

"I'm fine, Mom! Thanks for asking. But, I need to order some food and then I'll be heading to bed. So, I'll see you guys tomorrow."

"Okay! Bye honey", said my mom but she was not through.

"But oh yeah! Before I forget, Alyssa? Will Charles parents be there? And if so, where do you want us to meet them at?"

"Umm, no Mom. Unfortunately, they won't be there. They will be out of town for the next few days." I know she could sense the disappointment in my voice as I did hear hers as we hung up the phone. I shook my head and went back upstairs.

As I started to lay back down for some strange reason I began to feel my stomach rumbling.

"Hey Charles, let's go for a late night snack run. Or, by any chance, is there food in the fridge to cook?" I asked while holding my belly. "I'm hungry, who delivers around here? I wouldn't mind having pizza."

"Girl, it's 11:00 PM and everything is closed but if anything you could check the kitchen," Charles finally answered. "But I'm fine. I actually need to start doing these exercises to get prepared for tomorrow," he alerted. "And plus I definitely need to get some rest since I have to be up early in the morning."

Charles then slid out the bed, put on some boxer briefs and started to do his pushups on the floor. I couldn't help but notice his bulging muscles and tight abs as he then began to count his reps.

"Hmm," I thought to myself. The sight of his body always turned me on. The more he worked out, sweated, and flexed, the more I wanted him. My sex drive was increasing speedily as I watched him focus on alternating exercises and fought my own desires to distract him at those very moments.

He completed his routine and sat on the bed next to me. I could feel his intense body as he pulled me closer to him. I wiped the sweat from his forehead before he leaned in to whispered, "I love you," in my ear softly with a smile on his face. I replied the same and gave a quick peck on the lips then I insisted we showered before bed. With a devilish grin, he agreed.

As I quietly laid there I couldn't help but think back at how Charles was arguing with the cop. And the angry facial expression the officer made as we started to walk off. For some odd reason it just didn't *feel* right. The officer seemed sneaky, and overall wrong for the way he abused his power.

I only started to drift off after I caught a quick glimpse of the clock on the wall. There were only a few more hours left until

I had to be up with Charles to get ready to meet with my parents at his game.

So without further thought I finally shut my eyes and fell fast asleep.

"Good morning, everyone! It will be slightly cloudy with a slight chance of rain," the news reporter blared, the loud tone of his voice woke me up. Charles had the television volume up extremely high so it was the first thing I heard. Then I opened my eyes and seen the house was filled with smoke. In a few short seconds, the smoke alarm went off.

Scared, I quickly ran down the stairs and into the kitchen to see what all the smoke was coming from. To no surprise, Charles was in there making breakfast. Judging by the smoke, I could tell he had no clue what he was doing. I leaned against the fridge with a smirk on my face. I couldn't help but laugh seeing Charles dance with his back toward me and his headphones in his ears.

Eventually I reached over to tap him on his shoulder. His reaction was priceless. He jumped so high in the air, he ending up dropping the skillet he was using to make pancakes and sausages.

"Well good morning," I chuckled even though I tried to keep a straight face.

"Oh! Man, it's you!" Charles was startled. His eyes were wide and he holding his chest which made me laugh more.

"Well, I see you're up early! Do you mind opening some windows or the back door to let some of this smoke out?" I started to cough a bit as the combination of smoke and laughter became rather overwhelming. Charles, ignoring my melodramatics, instead went ahead and opened some windows.

As the coughing refused to let up, I started feel nauseous all over. I made my way to the bathroom to barf yet once again.

"Maybe there is something really wrong with me," I laid on the bathroom floor thinking to myself.

"Alyssa! Alyssa! Are you getting dressed?" Charles yelled loudly. "We need to be out the house in the next 20 minutes in order to make it to the game on time."

I reached up to the sink n while lifting myself up I started to feel a dizzy overwhelming feeling come over me. I stumbled slightly as I made my way to the bedroom and still managed to get dressed for the day's event.

We headed to the game I could see the nervousness on Charles' face as his forehead started to sweat as he stopped at a red light.

"Are you okay?" I asked.

"Yes, I'm totally fine, babe. And I'm sorry about breakfast. You hungry?" Charles asked although I was certain he already knew the answer.

"Yes… Extremely!"

We stopped at the drive-thru at a local breakfast spot. While pulling up to order, I noticed the same officer that harassed Charles walking out the exit door with his head held down. I took a deep breath and began to order my food.

"Now, are you okay?" Charles questioned. He whispered as if he was not trying to interrupt me speaking to the lady. It was not until after we pulled off with our food that I told Charles who I saw. Seeing his facial expression, I knew I had added more negativity to the thoughts already cycling through his mind.

"Man, forget him! I'm not worried at all. I know next time though, it won't be as nice for him." Charles grunted.

"Um, right! So what did you order?" I interrupted. It was clear Charles was getting more upset as he continued speaking on what he was going to do to the officer, should he see him again.

Ten minutes passed in silence and we finally pulled up to where the game was held. I was amazed by how big and crowded the stadium was as we then walked through the doors.

"Hey Alyssa", my mom and dad yelled across the lobby and waved us down. We walked over them as they hugged and greeted us in excitement.

"Well, I have to meet with my coach and team," Charles announced, "but before I leave, here are you guys' tickets." We all wished him luck and success for his big day. I squeezed tightly until he smiled and walked off toward the locker rooms.

I felt queasy now seating in the stadium's seats before the game. And felt even more uneasy as the announcer began to introduce all of the players to the field. But as soon as the announcer called Charles' name the feeling vanished instantly. I was so excited to see him as he walked through what seemed to be an entrance from the dugout.

The crowd went crazy holding up homemade signs and yelling his name. And just then, I noticed Charles mouth "I love you" like a whisper then blow a kiss in my direction. I blushed then returned the kiss which he caught before he walked back to the dugout.

As the game went on and the temperature dropped, I couldn't help but notice that the score was not even close. Charles and his team were almost up by double digits in the sixth inning.

Several seats down the aisle from where I was sitting sat an elder man writing in a notebook and talking on the phone. I smiled in hopes that it was the recruiter Charles was expecting to come especially since he was just as excited as I was, jumping up and down every time Charles was up to bat or hit a home run. I could only assume that it was good news that the potential recruiter was potentially relaying about Charles.

As the game ended with Charles' team winning 11-2 and the fans began to vacate the stadium, my family and I decided to wait for Charles in the lobby area. Charles exited the locker area with so much enthusiasm and greeted me the greatest hug he had ever given me. We all collected our belongings and headed out of the stadium as Charles informed us of his opinion of the game and his overall stats. We were all very happy for him.

"Good game, Charles," my dad congratulated while reaching in to shake his hand, "you're on your way pro."

"Thanks sir", Charles replied with the biggest smile on his face. I kissed my mom and dad good night and we split our separate ways to our cars.

"You know, you had a great game tonight," the recruiter yelled out from a distance across the parking lot. The elder man I had noticed earlier now walked toward us and shook Charles' hand.

"Oh, man! Mr. Edward, thanks, that really means a lot sir!"

"I hope you're ready for the draft day next week. You should be a high prospect. I'd say top 3, easily," the recruiter mentioned, obviously impressed.

"I sure can't wait Sir," Charles said with an exciting tone. The two of them shared a couple short exchanges more before shaking hands again and departing ways. When we got to the car Charles held my door open for me. Once I was in safe he got in on the driver's side, started the car and drove off. A smile never leaving his face.

Chapter 4

Draft day was finally here. I had witnessed overwhelming excitement fill Charles face each day since the big game as he prepared himself both mentally and physically for today's results. He had spent the last two months visiting various training camps all across America to see which team would best suit him and vice versa. But for some strange reason, as I laid there in my bed next to Charles and he still laid there sound asleep, something did not feel right.

"Wake up, honey", I whispered playfully in his ear. I touched on his chest and slightly nudged him thinking at the very least he would open his eyes. Instead, he just rolled over while pulling the rest of the covers, including the little I had over me, to his side of the bed.

"Fine then!" I said as I giggled and headed toward the bathroom.

As I began to run my bath water, I couldn't help but feel a strange nauseous feeling come over me as I then began to throw up just barely making it to the toilet. While pulling myself up and finally getting in the bathtub, I couldn't help but think over the possibility of me being pregnant. I shrugged it off initially but then thought, if I am pregnant, how would I tell my family? Most importantly, how would I tell Charles?

More thoughts poured into my mind before I decided I should go to the local Smith Mart and at least buy a pregnancy test before I continue with assumptions. However, the entire time got dressed I wondered in full anticipation of what the results will be.

I pulled up to the Smith Mart in my dad's car and immediately recognized the one officer that had assaulted Charles talking with a store patron in the parking lot. I refused to make eye contact with him as swiftly walked through the door with my head held low. From the corner of my eye I could see his eyes following me into the store.

"Excuse me, miss?" I said once I located the nearest Smith Mart employee. Slightly annoyed and impatient, I tapped her shoulder to get her attention. As she turned around, my feelings changed.

"Oh my freakin' goodness! Heyyyyy boo!" My older cousin Jada shouted in a surprising voice. I had not seen her in forever so I was definitely excited as well.

"Oh, my God, Jay! How are you?" We were so busy jumping up and down, smiling and hugging each other that my question went unanswered.

"What brings you here this early in the morning," she said with a curious look on her face. And then it hit me as I then began to feel nervous and kind of embarrassed to even tell her the real reason why I was there. So I tried to change the subject asking about her mom and family thinking it would work.

"Stop it girl," she interrupted with a smirk on her face. "What's the real reason you are here this morning?" She could sense that it was something serious.

"Talk to me girl, you know how close we use to be. Is it something you're hiding?" She asked.

Boom! My eyes almost popped out of their sockets as she hit the nail right on the head. It felt like a million tons of brick had hit me all at once. I felt my nerves rushing in and the back of my neck was getting strangely sweaty but I could not keep the *secret* in any longer.

"Well, yes," I said. With my head held low I confessed to her about the nausea and vomiting.

"Wait hold up, Miss Alyssa?" She said with a shocked tone in her voice. "Are you telling me you might be pregnant?"

"Well kind of, sort of," I said with a nervous giggle. "But if anything, can you point me to the pregnancy tests?"

"Oh, of course," she insisted while grabbing my hand and dragging me to the aisle where they were.

I stared over the brands while attempting to accept the fact that I *might* be a parent soon. There may be a little life growing inside of me right now. In a few short months, I will hold someone that calls me, Mommy.

I hurried those thoughts away and just selected the test that seemed the most efficient. Jada and I walked over to the register and she checked me out quickly. After paying, I stopped short of leaving as

I noticed what seemed to be the officer was still outside, now alone and just staring inside the store in my direction. Turned around to Jada and signaled for her to come over.

I told her all that occurred between "the officer" and Charles and she was shocked. She informed me that she never witnessed any issues like at the Smith Mart. She made it seem like the officer was a regular, harmless, friendly customer. She even called him by his first name, "Harris" but then she mentioned whenever there were problems it was usually a female that he got out of line with.

I frowned and while her version of that man seemed interesting, it was time for me to get back to Charles. Jada gave me her cellphone number and or insisted I called her cell or the store if I ever needed to talk to her about anything as I prepared myself to leave out.

I stepped about three feet out of the building before I felt a slightly aggressive tap on my shoulder.

"Congrats, Miss. I hope you found what you all needed today." My face screwed up as a turned to see this goofy, Rent-A-

Cop looking, parking lot security creep smiling at me. I felt better and worse knowing that it was him that had been staring at me the whole time.

"Thanks, I sure did," I said while nodding my head and hurrying to the car. I got in, locked the doors and headed home.

I raced into the bathroom after I peeked in the room to see that Charles was still asleep.

"Charles, wake up" I yelled to him while squatting over the toilet seat. I was finally taking a pregnancy test and the anxiety of it all was kicking in.

Only about thirty whole seconds went by before Charles knocked on the bathroom door.

"Babe, what are you doing?" He said. "I really have to use it."

"Okay! Here I come, calm down and give me a minute!" I replied with a nervous giggle as I flushed the toilet and turned on the water to muffle the sound of my gathering all of my trash and other belongings.

As I slowly made my way to the door and placed my hand on the knob, the results showed up. With a very surprised look on my face, I couldn't help but notice that it read "positive".

"Hurry up now, Alyssa", Charles demanded with a serious tone in his voice. So I finally opened the door and he quickly ran to the toilet.

"Happy now?" I said giggling.

I made my way to the room and quickly dressed all while still stunned that soon I will be a mom. But it was also Charles' Draft day today and I couldn't forget that. Both of our families had planned to meet at the Draft arena to accompany Charles on his big day. Then we were going to dinner to celebrate.

He came back into the room all relieved and started getting dressed. I could not make what song he was mumbling but I could clearly tell he didn't know all the words. As his singing got worse I decided I should interrupted him.

"So!" I said. "How was your sleep?" I asked, "Seemed like you slept well."

"It was okay", he replied. "But I rolled over and you wasn't there where did you go?" He enquired.

"Oh, no where! Just to the store to pick up a couple snacks", I said playfully. "Speaking of which," I quickly paused, changing the subject before he had the opportunity to ask for some, "guess who I ran into, staring me down over there?"

"Who?" Charles stopped everything and looked at me with his full attention. So I filled him in about Officer Norman, how he was watching me in the store, and then how I thought it was him still staring when I was trying to leave but it was Harris' creepy self.

To my surprised Charles didn't seem upset nor did he laugh it off or anything. He just took a deep breath and confirmed whether I was okay and asked if either of them tried to argue or harm me.

"No," I replied with a soft yet worried tone.

"It just seemed kind of weird, that's all," he stated. "But, we have better things to look forward to." He smiled and lighten up as he then began to tie his tie and straighten out his suit.

"Yea, you're right!" I agreed. "I just can't wait until tonight!"

I encouraged the mood and put a bright smile on my face along with my heels on my feet.

Charles look at my outfit and in approval said, "Me either!", as we both left out the room and headed down stairs.

You would have thought it was prom night the way my mom got excited to see us all dressed up. She actually made us stand in the middle of the living room and snapped several pictures before asking Charles if he was ready to for the results tonight.

"Yes ma'am, I'm 'bout as ready as ready can be." Charles gleamed.

"Well, either way, we're proud of you, Son", my dad said as he shook Charles' hand. He then picked up my mom's light coat and hurried her out the door. "We'll meet you guys there, drive safe!"

As we pulled out my drive way I couldn't help but get that overwhelming feeling that something bad was going to happen. The sky was gray though the birds were chirping; it just felt like somebody's parade would be rained on. Charles offered to drive because my dad told him a lady in heels should never have to drive herself anywhere. I smiled, but after a ten minute ride turned to twenty minutes, I started to wish we did not take my dad's instructions.

"Hey, Alyssa! Please turn on the GPS. For some reason I just got lost", Charles said jokingly. He made a sharp U-turn as I set the navigation in route.

No soon as we reached the speed limit did I see the flashing lights.

"Oh my god, please, Charles pull over."

Charles complied and directed the car onto the shoulder of the road. I could tell he was just as nervous as I was.

"What the hell is going on?" He mumbled under his breath.

Knock! Knock!

We both looked to the driver's side window and low and behold, Officer Norman stood before us. Charles, though instantly agitated, took a deep breath and swallowed hard prior to lowering his window.

"Excuse me Sir, is there an issue?" Charles asked.

Without answering his question Officer Norman gave us a stern and smug face, then he demanded to see the driver's license and registration for the car. From the tone of his voice you could tell the officer was up to no good.

Charles slowly reached into his wallet for his license as I passed him the registration papers from the glove compartment.

He handed the documents to the authority expressing more concern, "What's the problem Sir?"

Again, he was ignored as the officer took the items to his patrol car. He then shortly after returned without the documents and requested that Charles stepped out of the car.

"Excuse me?" Charles asked with a serious tone in his voice.

"Step out the car now!" The officer became aggressive, slamming his balled fist on the roof of the car.

The sound startled us both.

"Charles, please just get out the car and do what he tell you," I said as tears began to fall from my eyes.

Charles opened the car door and slowly began to step out the car. The officer then snatched Charles by the arm and threw him against the hood of the car.

"No!" I yelled at the top of my lungs. "What is going on, Officer Norman?" I screamed as I got out of the car in Charles defense. "Please! Leave him alone!"

I could feel myself crying harder now. "Please! What did he do?"

Charles was furious being pinned to the car while I begged for Officer Norman to let him go. However, the officer instructed me to get back in the car and they began to tussle. Officer Norman, having the clear advantage, hit Charles in the face.

"What did I do?" Charles cried with rage. Again, with no answer, the officer struck Charles for the second time. Charles began to fight back, landing in a few good blows. He even somehow snagged the officer's name badge.

"Oh no, you done messed up now! You think you're tough big guy?" The officer asked loudly. He tripped Charles, punched him heavy in the face and then football punt kicked him in the chest. Charles laid there helplessly. "Not so tough now?"

I immediately called 911 for an ambulance.

"Please help! My boyfriend just got beat up by an officer. Norman is his last name and my boyfriend is lying there unconscious. He's not moving. Please!" I gave them the location pinpointed on the navigation system then rushed out the car in attempt to aid Charles.

Realizing what he'd done, Officer Norman retreated to his police car and left the scene before the ambulance arrived. *That coward.*

I called my dad, "Dad, please help!" I cried.

"What, Alyssa? Where are you?" He said with a very concerned tone.

"We were just assaulted by a dirty cop, please come. Charles is hurt," I sobbed. Tears where falling so wildly from my face I could barely see. Then out of nowhere, sharp pains shot through my abdomen and chest and I dropped the phone. I could hear my dad asking for our location while the ambulance arrived but all I could think of was my baby. I still had to tell Charles about *our* child.

I blacked out during the ride to the hospital but woke up at the entrance in a wheelchair with blood all over me from holding Charles' limp body in my arms. I asked for a checkup after they rushed Charles into the emergency operating room.

"Are you okay, Alyssa?" My dad ran in out of nowhere and began to hold me. I broke down into rapid tears again.

"Everything just happened so—"

"Excuse me," a nurse interrupted, "please follow me to the doctor," she insisted as she guided us to a hospital room. "The doctor will be there shortly."

I nodded with appreciation as a tried to calm my emotions.

"What is going on?" My dad was worried and confused but my hesitation was not making the situation better.

"Where is Mom?" I questioned, noticing her absence.

"She is still at the draft arena seated. I have to call her and update her with all that is going on. But don't change the subject. Why are you being checked in to the hospital?" He asked with a serious tone in his voice. "Did he hit you? Are you okay?"

I shook my head, no, and motioned to put on the hospital gown given to me by the nurse prior to leaving. My dad accepted my response, for that moment, and stepped out of the room and walked down the hall to give me privacy.

"Hello, Alyssa?" The doctor entered shortly after, reading my name off my clipboard. "My name is Dr. Brianne Peterson and I am here to give you a quick check up. I see you were involved in an accident, was it? Is anything specifically bothering you right now?" The doctor asked many questioned all of which I answered truthfully and thoroughly. She examined my body based on my responses and in all it only lasted ten short minutes.

Before she left I asked her to turn the TV on to the Smith Network as the draft had already started. I had already missed the first two picks but more than that, I was wondering how Charles was. I hoped that Charles was okay.

My dad finally returned with an awkward smile. He then informed me that Charles had been drafted by the Smithville Cougars in the second round which was amazing. Charles would finally have the opportunity to play for his dream team.

My dad also said the police located Officer Norman and was arrested on drunk driving, assault and battery, and other charges. Officer Norman had been under investigation for abusing his authority and assaulting others prior to tonight.

"Wow, I hope he rots in jail, Dad. Charles didn't deserve any of this! But I'm still so happy for him. I guarantee he will be pleased as soon as he hears the news. Did the doctors say anything you about his condition?"

He shook his head.

As the night went on my mom and Charles' parents finally came to the hospital.

"How are you feeling?" My mom worried with a nervous look on her face.

"I'm fine, just stomach pains," I replied.

I told them all the scene by scene replay of Charles and the officer. I could see the frustration and sadness in everyone's faces as I began to cry again. My mom cuddled me as I tried to get myself together. Charles' mom passed me some tissue to wipe my face.

I was almost emotionless when the small team of doctors came into my room with their heads hanging less than high and reluctantly sighing.

"What's the matter, Doc'?" My dad and Charles' dad rose to their feet.

"Umm, we do have some very disturbing news," one of the doctor's spoke after assuring Charles' parents were present. I grabbed my covers tight and began to cry as I was certain the inevitable was coming. My mom looked my direction and rubbed my back as hugged and attempted to console me again.

"Due to severe injuries Charles suffered from wrestling with the officer including a cracked skull, broken ribs, and a punctured lung, he succumbed to his wounds at 10:38PM this evening."

Everyone in the room cried at that moment.

I struggled to speak at first but once I toned my emotions down I somehow gathered everyone's attention. With tears still in my eyes, I held my mom and Charles' mom's hand in mine and professed how much I loved everybody in that room, including Charles. Though he was not there, he was ultimately the reason we were all in the same place at that time.

"And since we are all in here together," I mentioned after wiping my tears so I could look everyone in their face clearly, "I'm pregnant."

The End !

"Lilly's Adventure"
Written by: Lauren M. Smith

There was a little girl name Lilly who's
birthday was right around the corner. One day
after school her and her mother went shopping
at the mall. As they looked through the different
stores together somehow Lilly got lost. She then
started to panic as tears begin to fill her eyes.

while looking for her mom she ran into a little boy named john.

"Hi, are you ok"? John asked.

"No I'm not, I just lost my mom", Lilly replied as she tried to hold back from crying.

Well I can help you find her just follow me. As they both looked around the mall looking for Lilly's mom, they ran across a sign that said "Santa's work shop", that was right ahead.

They then begin to follow the different signs that led to where Santa was sitting. They both got in line to take pictures. Then it was Lilly's turn to sit on Santa's lap.

"Hi little lady", Santa Claus said.

"What would you like for Christmas"?

While looking down she then asked if Santa can help find her mom.

"Ok little girl", Santa replied I will help you find her in no time.

He then called over his little elves and whispered in their ears about what the problem had been.

They quickly paged her over the intercom and before you know it Lilly's mom was standing right there with a smile on her face as they both continued shopping the whole day. They then went home and lived happily ever after.

The end!

REST IN PEACE

DAMARKUS & STONEY